T0359729

THE OPEN
LUCY VAN

Other publications by Lucy Van

AUDIO
Figures

LUCY VAN

THE OPEN

CORDITE BOOKS

First printed in 2021
by Cordite Publishing Inc.

PO Box 393
Carlton South 3053
Victoria, Australia
cordite.org.au | corditebooks.org.au

© Copyright Lucy Van 2021
© Introduction copyright Merlinda Bobis 2021

Lucy Van and Merlinda Bobis assert their right to be known as the
respective author and introducer of this work.

National Library of Australia
Cataloguing-in-Publication:

   Van, Lucy
   The Open
   978-0-6489176-0-1 paperback
   I. Title.
   A821.3

Poetry set in Spectral 10 / 14
Cover design by Zoë Sadokierski
Text design by Kent MacCarter and Zoë Sadokierski
Printed and bound by McPherson's Printing, Maryborough, Victoria.

Supported by the City of Melbourne Arts Grants Program and the
City of Melbourne COVID-19 Arts Grants.

All rights reserved.

This book is copyright. Apart from any fair dealing for the purposes of
research, criticism, study, review or otherwise permitted under the
Copyright Act, no part of this book may be reproduced by any process
without permission. Enquiries should be addressed to Cordite
Publishing Inc. Cordite Publishing Inc. thanks Merlinda Bobis,
Penelope Goodes and Lucy Van for their input during the production
and editing of this book.

10 9 8 7 6 5 4 3 2

CONTENTS

PREFACE

The old hill near where I grew up was outwardly ruined: its pines were dead, its vines gone to seed and its sheds, which once held some purpose, sunk and rusted. With my immature logic I considered this place open and powerful, even though the land was enclosed by a wire fence and fallow from overcultivation and neglect. Like other places in the world, the traces of colonial settlement here held dull, sour feelings. The entire place seemed displaced from itself; maybe nothing could belong there.

Writing these poems has something to do with being in lands like this. As a child that hill gave me my first feeling of personal privacy, even though it was open, even though it was fenced for someone else, and perhaps because the fence was there. The poems here express indignation at the eventual consequences of privacy. Yet, equally, privacy fascinates me. Equally, fences fascinate me – their lines, their tensions, their bending. I am not the first to say that poetry is a form of enclosure, but I want to say it here again, anyway. I love how permeable this form of enclosure can be. In the same way, I loved how the fence around that private hill would bend as I moved through it.

INTRODUCTION

This door, this *though*

All doors are open in Lucy Van's poetry. Ingress and egress are multiple, even coincident. We've just touched *what's here*, or are about to touch it, when apprehension is quickly unsettled, halted or reconfigured. Because we're only passing through a door or another door is opening, as the poet offers: 'Another thought though (and oh, I think about how thought and though are very similar words)'. Hers is a liminal *though*. Between what's touched and what's yet to be touched. Site of frisson. Contention. Then insight.

The book opens to Hotel Grand Saigon: 'I have gone back and now I am here.' 'Back' is her father's family and roots in Vietnam, opening the door to his migration history, only a peek, though ('Never write a poem about a boat'), then opening to Vietnam's colonial history. And now we are here where the Vietnamese staff 'are always ready to serve' the French and other holidaying Europeans and white Australians, and herself, the Vietnamese Australian poet 'coming home', *though* also waited on or waiting in a gift shop and unable to ask, because she can't speak her father's language. Van's poetry is an ongoing decolonial passage. Each opened space and time takes to task the one just left, then comes home to the poet, her self-reflexive *though* pointing to her own entanglement. She's inside and outside these pasts and presents, or presences: touched and untouched.

But is one ever untouched? The ocean passes beneath these poems and one inevitably gets wet. It's 'a liquidation of territory', whether in Vietnam or in Australia, where land has been liquidated, too, by the passage of colonial ships through water. Public or personal territory, even the most intimate, is persistently liquidated. Disappeared by coloniality, modernity, progress, by growing up and outgrowing, or by an aside, this *though*. Or simply made liquid, flowing through the next door, only to reappear as something else at the other side before moving on again. Van's quicksilver to-ing and fro-ing creates an insight-coaxing discombobulation. But it's the liquidation of the poem's territory that is the hallmark of this collection, prose poems occasionally juxtaposed with the familiar shape: that block of a poem. To accentuate the liquidation? These prose poems start as a moment flowing in interior monologue into multiple spaces and times. Then sneakily, and bravely too, they open estranging doors, so poetry starts reading like short story becoming extemporaneous discourse, erudite and interrogative, hopscotching from Foucault to Kristeva to Homer to Bishop to Whitman to Catullus to Malouf to Plath.

Each is a new door opening: this *though*.

Is this from the sheer force of water that wants out, wants more?

The poet's serve is vigorous: reader hurtles through another door and is suddenly in the middle of the Australian Open. Here, '[t]he court is [her] discursive space'. The 'serve is the rhetorical question' and the return, birdsong, 'the aggressive claiming of territory'. Or merely a wish to restore what was liquidated? Tennis becomes philosophy. The line of thought is the line of *though*: one is again taken elsewhere. But always she returns to family, home, the intimate, the body touched and untouching: 'most of your life you are coming home ... all the while you are leaving'. It's when Van is in this transit on 'A Little Cloud' that she's most moving, and she transcends. Like when she watches her father drink a Fanta – poet drinking him up down to 'the lump in his throat mechanical with thirst' – and she's 'transposed ... to the temple', to '[p]laces like this ... filled with doors'.

—Merlinda Bobis

HOTEL
GRAND
SAIGON

I

I have gone back and now I am here.

This is a colonial swimming pool. I'm facing a lifeguard's chair and a lifesaver, and they are both ornamental. There is some sort of hook near these ornaments. Earlier today at my cousin's wedding I saw my dad's cousin, Chú Cau, who lived with us at some stage in Australia. It felt like he had come back for good.

According to my sister he used to look after us when we were little. I remember him as a presence discovered in the backyard. The story was simple: he was handsome and bright until he drowned in a pool as a child. It was in colonial Saigon and nobody could swim. There was a photograph of his mother, my dad's aunt, sitting in front of what might have been a totally different colonial pool or might have been that one. It could have been taken before or after the drowning. I always thought the photo was taken while it was happening. What happened next is a separate story.

Chú Le, my dad's brother, telling me how the American GIs used to come to the house to speak to him and my dad when they were kids, because the two of them learned English listening to BBC radio.

This was something I hadn't known. 'Your English is really good,' I tell him; I'm being patronising. It's true. He hasn't spoken English for 40 years, he tells me. Not since the end of the war. 'Your English is good,' I tell him. 'Really?' he asks.

With all the help in the world I've been learning French for a year or more and I have no idea what this French family on the next banana lounges down are saying. Like no idea. But I speak English really well. I speak English really well. My English is really good.

II

Another thought though (and oh, I think about how thought and though are very similar words), being here at the Hotel Grand Saigon pool: so, this is what you guys are up to. By this I mean holding but not really reading Vietnam travel guides, dozing phone in other hand on banana lounges, or rousing and calling for towels; by you guys I mean the Europeans and the white Australians; by up to I mean when you say you're on holiday in Vietnam.

Oh what can I say – I am jealous over these bodies and these languages. The confidence with which one can call for a towel. There's nothing else I think these guys should be doing in this French colonial hotel. Oh what can I say about the throwback. Because there are definitely French people here. And this is definitely a French colonial hotel, staffed by Vietnamese service staff. The service staff are never seen on break. They are always ready to serve.

And I had wanted to know my father, the source of all this money and anxiety.

And I was careful and overcalculated my address.

III

This is a single-use plastic drink bottle. For a plastic it is soft and it makes a soft and crumpled cadence in my hand and as I drink from it, it makes an O and I make an O. Later, Dad drains his drink bottle, crumples it, leaves it on the seat of a stranger's motorbike.

I always enjoyed watching him drink things out of cans: Fanta, Coke, Solo. I would watch him working in the long backyard, on his day off, pushing the lawnmower. I would listen and wait for it to pull. I would walk out with a drink fresh from our fridge. He would stop and stand, the lump in his throat mechanical with thirst.

I'm standing at the Stelae of Scholars. Thinking, obviously. Implying the stupidity of duration. Always be implying. Later, I will be standing in the gift shop.

In that ingenious way of his he had transposed me to the temple, to its beaten apprentices and sacred doors. Why this interest in doors, other than the existence of so many of them. Places like this, places outdoors, filled with doors.

IV

When I burn electrodes my shoulders burn and my shirt explodes and everything is on fire. Uncle Tuong didn't fight back but sat on the floor and took off his shirt and cried. This is a narrative detail. Our family is working class, we all insist: 'I said you better lay down on the road so I can run you over myself. Because if you stay like that, you're better off dead.' It was the gentle brother who was the hard drinker; it was the other who abstained. I don't know why I want to tell you this. I abhor violence and I have also acquired a taste for it. This is my absurd vengeful gratitude.

Don't reason with me. Carefully select the correct doors. The significance of the Stelae, with the scholars' names inscribed in stone on the backs of turtles. They are doctors and they are poets. I mean the doctors were the poets, these things were the same things. I give my concerned son 200,000 dong to take back to the gift store.

He hands me something. It's the only souvenir we will have of this trip. It is a heavy plastic thing and it is sitting in a hand. A gold patina model after the Stelae – on the back of a turtle. On the Stelae – smudged – my name in his writing. It keeps coming off.

V

I find myself reading *Civilisation and Its Discontents*. I am still by the pool. I now do nothing for myself because the workers do everything for me. I watch myself not working and I watch the workers working. They are waiters, their work is to wait. Or they are servers, and their work is to service. To serve this cosmic tact. I am aware that this is this way because I am from a rich country. I am from a rich country because I was smuggled over from this poor one. The valise was carefully stowed in the most tactfully cosmic of places. When I came here, I had a soft bag packed with Freud, Adorno and the diaries of Ned Rorem, that inspired bitch. I am aware of the contents of this bag. All this is an antithetical act.

Nobody watches the Hopman Cup, which plays in the corner of the outdoor bar. Suppose there is something foolish about the public voice.

My father hates our sweet talk. He arranges his flowers carefully. Catullus: 'Like an Asian myrtle-bush / shining bright with flowering twigs'.

Never write a poem about a boat. In fact, never translate and never use metaphors. Never use verse to pray for the sight of land nor record the anguish of typhoon season. This is when you leave because no one expects escape under these conditions.

For example, never say 'we are foam'. Never say 'we drown'.

VI

most of your life you are coming home
you turn the last corner
look for the blue fence blue roof

all the while you are leaving
you try to remember
the word 'exposition'

most of you left in headwind
'suddenly' an adverb
best applied to tides

the ocean on a roll today
rolling for conversations
lapping at revelations

establishing shots on the rocks
staring back like
listening to the words like

waving containing
docking stripping
attacking rolling smoko

VII

This became our regular walk around Hoàn Kiếm. When I looked later on the map, I saw that it was a very indirect and impractical route. By going this way, we missed many places of significance. For example, by going this way we didn't see the gatehouse to the former Hoả Lò prison, but saw instead Hanoi Tower, which was on the side facing Quán Sứ, the third road we took.

Đường Lê Duẩn (left). Lý Thường Kiệt (left). Quán Sứ (right). Hàng Bông (which becomes Hàng Gai). *Popeyes*.

VIII

Still running, Daphne cried out to her father, 'Change me!' and we came, that was all part of our plan, we were expected to come to the house and to spend a few days and nights there, that was all a big part of it but it turned out that there was this difficulty and this problem and just when we thought there would be introductions

he left and we could not sense what it was going to be like and I didn't know the name of the aunt on the hospital bed so I didn't know how to ask if she was ok or if there was something I could do and I didn't want to waste everybody's time with all my questions because it seems like that's all I had, questions and time, and it had happened before, my cousin said,

'When I first saw you, I hated you,' and the reason I never learnt the language was no one ever taught me and maybe that's a mental illness thing, not a migration thing, and it's all a big joke when one of my uncles points a finger into my shoulder and says, with a deliberate pause: 'I hear you are a doctor, of poetry!'

When we were there we didn't know where to be but maybe that was because we didn't want to be there but hadn't we been looking forward to it? We were in the way at the shop in the front with the door to the street kept wide open so sometimes I thought relatives were my aunties' customers and we were taking up room in the room

behind that bit because everyone kept getting up when we tried to join them watching television and staring at the bananas and I didn't know what the way was to get a glass of water because it always seemed wrong or rude, very rude, way past the kitchen so we just stayed in bed

he built this house and oh I don't understand the back of the house, no, we didn't have a rich experience, that's your thing, we slipped away.

IX

Not so near the Continental Palace Hotel, which Graham Greene monumentalised, a little closer to Saigon Post Office, where Duong Van Ngo, the last public letter writer, is still at work; about a 30-minute walk straight down Xô Viết Nghệ Tĩnh from our family's house; near the school that was formerly the Collège de jeunes filles indigènes; adjacent to the Jardin de la ville which was made after French settlers were encouraged to take exercise, Cercle Sportif was charging 500 piastres for annual membership when it relocated here in 1905. By 1926 one could confidently assert that Saigon had a club worthy of a colony. Elegant balls were held yearly, hosted at the Continental. The South Vietnamese politician Dương Văn Minh visited in the 1960s. He was known to be a skilful tennis player.

X

Later the Cercle Sportif becomes the Labour Culture Palace. For anyone who thinks with their ears, Cercle Sportif becomes Circle K, a business on a mission to take care of people's time.

This is private terminology. 'We are on a mission to take care of people's time.' It has something to do with the ability to arrive and leave. You're never there long unless invited by someone more permanent.

Only indirectly the woman chooses her own work. When she walks into the back of the shop, I don't know how to ask her to come back.

XI

Because I can't ask anyone and because I must leave everyone intact.
Or because I prefer not to ask.

XII

Vincom has the cleanest windows in the world. We have a beautiful, clean centre. We take photos of ourselves in front of the windows of Giordano, Furla, Aldo. In front of the windows of H&M. In front of the windows of Marks & Spencer.

Historical records show that we were born into a poor family. Due to accurate warehouse management and payroll, we have Wrap and Roll, Mochi, Mango, Bossini, Gucci. Due to construction management, we have windows, walls, floors, miracles.

XIII

The day after we have dinner at Vincom, I ask Tri if his mum likes cake. That morning I had seen cakes at a shop called Tous Les Jours, which is also in Vincom, on the basement level B2. I could get a whole cake, I reasoned, or an assortment of smaller cakes. What should I get her as a departing gift, I mean. In soft, careful English, he says, 'Just say goodbye,' which I know as soon as he says it I won't do.

Tri the same afternoon mooning around our hotel with its emperor's bed – made of two king-sized beds pushed together – says, 'I feel sad because I think you didn't have a good time here.'

I am so embarrassed about the size of the bed. He looks out of the window and tells me he lives somewhere far from District 1.

XIV

An early Vietnamese historian characterised his people as
intellectually inferior to the French, capable of great imagination in
the literary sphere but weak in the superior procedures of reason. I
didn't know until I lived in France that it was possible my father's
name, Loi, is not Vietnamese. Not pronounced Loi as in 'boy', but
'lwah', as in *noir*, or *soir*. Maybe everyone has been saying it wrong.
I haven't checked this with him, because we don't speak much, and
because when we do, the conversations are so terrible. So full of
the procedures of reason. Sometime during that first month over
there I came across his name, or rather the word for his name, in the
paperwork for the visa processes we were obliged to follow, because
loi is the French for law. Dad was born in 1954, the same year Vietnam
proclaimed its independence after defeating the French in the Anti-
French Resistance War. In the West, it's called the First Indochina
War. His legal papers record a different date of birth, for a completely
different day and month in the year 1955.

I don't know what his parents thought about the French, or what they
thought about Vietnam, or what they thought of independence. Was
that a big year for the law, 1954?

One of the things I do know about is that my father's father was a
famous chef in Saigon, both during and after French rule. He was a
celebrity.

That he seldom spoke is one of the legends about him. That he
seldom spoke was the point. For comparative purposes, my own
father is garrulous, like his mother, I think. These words create their
own opacity.

XV

One of the few things my grandfather, my Ông nội, said to my father when he was a child was 'never be a chef'. This is a shame, my father says, that his father was never proud of his acclaim, and he never sought to pass on his brilliant career to his sons. We are all proud that people still come to the house, seeking clarification on his recipes. They are French recipes, and it is a source of private pride to me that this quiet man, whom I only met once, sailed to Paris in his youth to learn how to cook. I like to think about the part in history when the colonial youth sails to Paris.

Unlike his mother, and unlike his siblings, my dad would wait, he told me, every night for his father to come home after working at whichever famous restaurant or hotel. While everyone else was in bed, they would go out for noodles. Once Ông nội was to be employed cooking for the president of South Vietnam. And my father asked his father, one night over noodles, whether he would slip some poison into the president's meal.

But I always thought I was to call him Up nội. That's what my ear gave my memory. But google 'up nội' and you get this translation: 'put the pot upside down'.

Or was it that he didn't want to cook for the president because going through all the doors required too much paperwork.

I wonder if it was the Continental Palace, or the Chinese-owned Majestic, or the Rex Hotel.

XVI

What insecurity and doubt lurk behind supremacy? There is *l'amour-propre* but there is also vexation. There is *l'amour de l'autre*. And maybe somewhere there is Ông nội, working on those glamorous riverboats, working in Saigon's immense colonial hotels, so welcoming of writers and entertainers, in those palaces, tired and silent, tall and handsome into his eighties, bad with money, whose name I have never been told. There is too much paperwork. I like to think about the time he really did name one of his middle children after the law. An ahistorical desire. He passed and named (what or who) in an attitude of ambivalence, with love and hatred. It's fading and renovating. It's the Hotel Grand Saigon.

XVII

Who brought you to the ocean? Who brought you from the fields to the ocean?

The moorings disappear into the bottom of the ocean. This place is running at a high cost, nowhere near the coast. Sometimes it is anchored, sometimes it is built into the ocean floor. Underwater erosion.

Take off your shirt. Is this your protest? Because you like it here. Because its surface is the surface of both worlds. Oh, the bathroom opens to the kitchen, that's a little different. That's correct, if you have nothing to hide, you have nothing to fear. That's correct, for efficiency purposes, most of the time you're awake on this platform. Most of the time you work. Each day here is different. But say that each day here is the same. In this way, each day has no history. In this way, desire.

There are abundant resources and labour. Did you long for escape? Shall we leave you intact? To save on cost, the managers are onshore making decisions. The operational staff are here, and they are divided into three groups: production, maintenance and service.

THE
ESPLANADE

I

'The only thing I am sorry about,' she said, 'is that so many of the photographs came back clear. When a negative cannot be restored it comes back clear.'

Some memories are clearer than others. Some come back clear. Some of the clearest memories involve the ocean.

Sitting where the land is cleared out by the waves of the Indian Ocean, alone or with my mother. It is a clear memory.

Waters clear the land. This place where the land is always cleared by water is called the beach. The sound here is the thump and the hiss of waves. A liquidation of territory. Only a little liquidation. All the territory must be eventually restored. But still, the sound does not relent, it is the sound of the ocean clearing land away, and I never heard it put back.

I have never been back. I will never put this back.

I don't understand it but when the water is white there is an electrical current running through the air that is trapped in the water. There is always a charge.

Sometimes I saw some of it put back, on mornings full of large, strange weeds left on the shore.

If I thought that there was a wind from the west, I thought of Africa. But I didn't exactly think Africa, more specifically I thought of the interval between this land and the next land, which is Africa. The interval is still clear to me. Its light dances. Somewhere the interval ends and it's Africa.

Somewhere a little further out, seals mate like sun kings on their private rock, and the light obviously dances.

And I have always felt sorry for people who didn't grow up next to an ocean, who couldn't find a similar kind of privacy, the privacy of this interval.

What was said. My mother: 'The ocean is never the same.' My mother: 'I swam with dolphins today.' My mother: 'Shall we walk a little further?' My mother: 'Shall we go back?'

And every time: 'The Pacific Ocean is so different to the Indian Ocean.' Looking at an ocean while remembering an ocean.

The strange Belle-Époque building housed tea-rooms above an un-Proustian fish and chip shop. Wishing for a Fanta. Waiting near the change rooms. She always takes so long. A window without glass facing the ocean. Stand there wet. Standing there wet at this window is the way to see the ocean. The building has a basement and an upstairs but has no real interior. There is nothing inside.

II

I mean, there was something so romantic about that part of the city.
Called the Esplanade, which can't explain anything: nothing was
there, even though people lived there, but after the streets and the
buildings there was all this grass in the dark right down to the river,
it was always empty and it was always night and nothing was there.
All memory out of order when it comes to all this lawn in stretched
proportions psychedelic: playing soccer for a team (how? why?) in
high school, chatting up the opposition, comes after playing frisbee
coming down off acid with Cameron, whose first apartment out of
home was down there, come to think of it, where he played drums
and his housemate was as good a friend as any of us at the time but
he somehow got edited out of collective memory. I or we sent the
housemate a spinach and ricotta roll in the mail, for no reason other
than to see if the post would deliver it. Checking out the bedsit with
Ben when it was time for him to move out of his place in Tuart Hill
comes before the first time I ever went to his house in Tuart Hill.
When I sat on his bed and it was afternoon, and I don't think I'd been
in Tuart Hill before, and even though it was like, he was a nice guy, he
had totally been waiting for a moment like that and I had no idea but
I was so easy when it came to sleeping with friends.

The bedsit was the Esplanade and from now on all bedsits are the
Esplanade. It was a furnished bedsit and the art deco building is
obviously now enlarged by desires 100 storeys high, priapic and
curved, like all buildings on the Esplanade, maybe for the light, the
river right there in the dark if you wait and does anyone even find
places like that anymore because I think I would take any of them.
Orange doilies. Brown ceramics. One copper lamp. One wooden
armchair. Table nest. A single bed. A print of a boat. Good day. He
nearly took it. I came with him. And after we saw it together we must
have decided to move in together because the next memory is of him
and me in the apartment in Murray Street. And the next memory is
of him speaking to another guy on the phone telling the guy to stop
calling and that no one in this situation was to be considered a friend.

And then the next memory is of coming over to his house in Tuart Hill, where the floorboards were dust-free and his housemate, who owned the place even though he was 23, talked about rendering the front and putting pressed metal in the kitchen. It was afternoon and then dusk then and it was dusk when we looked at the bedsit on the Esplanade.

The Esplanade where Marwah and I drank with that mob that was always down there and when the cute guy propositioned me I worried I was somehow being racist when I said I have a boyfriend even though I did. There was some sort of winter garden hothouse involved with the Esplanade. But it doesn't get cold in Perth. So it was incongruous but also essential and also like the Louvre but also like Perth.

The Esplanade where this complete idiot who we all knew for years squatted in a communal laundry in a deco apartment block and owned the only key to the bolt on the laundry door and he was way older than all of us which only bothers me right now and he wore eyeliner but not in a good way and devised banalities and stole my skateboard and even though neither of us could use it properly it was a point of contention. Something about fellating a chandelier. Later memory which was from a few years before, waiting to be let in to the apartment of two guys my first boyfriend was trying to befriend and smoking weed with them and them talking about music magazines with MPCs on the cover and talking about MPCs as the guitars of the future and me never saying a word and then the boys not letting us in that last time and then them telling that boyfriend they hated me.

The Esplanade where a few years ago every time we took psychedelics or smoked weed a group of us would wander til dawn, where a beautiful older woman who was probably 25 gave me a frangipani ('here is a frangipani') at 4 a.m. leaving the club together and I offended her a year later by telling someone else she came on too strong that time with the frangipani and she told me, while I handed her her drink over the bar of the club, 'sorry, *am I coming on too strong?*' I had no idea then but I was weirdly beautiful at 18, 19, not reassuringly but weirdly, it brought about intense encounters that I assumed to be a normal part of growing up. Ben, years later, when it was over and totally fucked, when I came to his house while visiting Perth, the house that Gail Jones rented once (according to the mail he had to redirect), crying because I'd just seen my sister's dog run over and it was basically my fault for crossing the road irresponsibly and it was close enough to our childhood house that my dad came running or was he chasing my death away. Me crying and Ben and then Ben undressing me and then after saying, 'I just wanted to know how it feels to be the other guy.'

The Esplanade where we sat staring as the water police tried to coax a drunk out of the river. Hiding behind a pylon or buoy or boat. Relieved because for a few minutes earlier though it comes to me later we wondered why on earth we'd chosen to walk here because it seemed like just as we came he drowned.

III

I was already out of home several years or so I thought then and I was living with a lovely young man, etc., who was involved with music, etc. Even then I wanted to be a writer and occasionally said so. It was a time when I wore something on my sleeve, don't know what it was but I don't wear it anymore. Men used to see it. There was a man I would see sitting in cafes in the city where this apartment was, still is, and he would always see me. It wasn't a bad city. The man was much older and maybe from a city in Spain. I'm more than not sure. He said his name once and maybe it was Emmanuel. He always smiled at me and I smiled back. Benevolent nature. Or to keep him at bay. Benvolio? He said he was a writer and could I help him edit his story. Maybe I was working at that university press at this time, which may have made me feel like this was something I could do for someone like Benvolio. I don't remember the story but I remember sitting in that beautiful little apartment with him. It was a converted apartment, maybe one of the earlier ones in that city. The building was once a Salvation Army congregation hall. In the apartment there were no doors but the front and the back doors and there were these massive arched windows. Arches. People passing. And though it had little floor space it had a huge ceiling. Is that right? I mean, the space between floor and ceiling was: oh my god. I lived with this lovely man who I loved. His grandmother had a childhood in Western Australia that she famously never talked about. I wonder, Sister Kate's? His unusual soul? I never told him about Bennett Street. The Spanish man knew about this man but never met him or maybe he did. All I remember about Emmanuel's story is how he put it into my desktop computer, which was on my desk with a map of the world on it in professional laminate. The USSR in rose. I was pretty young, despite what I said earlier. The desk was near the door. The front door, so that if anyone came in they would see who was on the computer and what they were doing straight away. It would be the first thing they would see. I sat and looked at his story, typing (what?) while he cried out in protest whenever I mistyped anything, which was often, and his head was as close to the screen and the keyboard as mine. Gabriel?

It was annoying but I found myself just agreeing with whatever this man wanted me to do. I read somewhere that bad writing is universal. He was always sitting at cafes or maybe they were McDonalds or maybe they were Hungry Jacks. It was Hay Street Mall and it was Murray Street Mall. Once we were walking together in one of the two city malls and a guy asked him for change and the Spanish man said, 'I don't have any change,' and then the man pointed to the Spanish man's drink, a 600ml bottle of Coke, and said, 'Can I have a sip,' and the Spanish man said, 'That's my drink, man.' The other man didn't ask me for anything. Not anything at all. The Spanish man asked once to see my writing and I showed him something, which was a description of an apartment building that had just been built. The builders had finished it. But it was empty. There were no occupants. From the narrator's point of view the building was black, reflecting the river at night, which was what it faced and in fact what the whole city faces. I should know its name by now. Maybe there was a light on. There was probably one light on. Somewhere in the building. Somewhere in the middle. Or the bottom. Or the top. The Spanish man said, 'Hey man, that's ok,' but that's not a story. That's not how you tell a story.'

IV

I was thinking about producing discomfort.

I was curious about one thing, though I am very light with Cameron, which is not to say I don't get pissed off or randomly moody when I'm with him. But I have literally never tallied things for or against him. And come to think of it he often took me to the airport when I first started going to Sydney all the time, which is to say when I fell for Leo. In the car on the return leg between Wangi Falls and Darwin I realised I was quite sad, sadness about leaving the Falls, which incidentally went from one to three nights pretty seamlessly, touched something else and I dug into my bag for that inevitable valium when I realised I couldn't kick the mood, even with Cameron pulling the car over to correct the music situation (he found a proper house mix) and telling me about his friend Kyran, who I may have met many times. Cameron gave me lots and lots of backstory. I looked at the little grass trees and other flora unnameable right now, eating muesli from a box with my hand because we'd lost the spoon. At some point near Batchelor I said something along the lines of, 'I'm really emotionally blocked at the moment,' which is and isn't an unusual thing for me to say to Cameron, and he changed the subject pretty quickly, which is standard and correct in terms of our deal as friends. He said we'd return to that topic and I didn't mind not returning at all, and I mulled over what I said and just thought to myself, 'I have no idea what the problem is,' and I said to Cameron a few minutes later, 'Leo and I still haven't discussed what that trip was.' And I had to clarify I meant France and Cameron said, 'You should definitely have that talk while drunk,' and I thought that was a great point and at some point my valium must have kicked in and then we neared the outskirts of Darwin. On the plane now I can't quite picture that drink happening. I think I should write a glossary of terms from our trip: effective (which Cameron hated) to designate when something was good. I believe by the second-last day there was some sort of policy in place whereby I was limited to a maximum of five 'effectives' per day, which was harder than it sounds, but eventually led to the creation or renaissance of 'correct': 'correctivism' was the hangman word of our very lazy iced coffee at the cafe/ information shelter at Wangi that by this point felt like part of our house, or rather a very good place to lie down on a bench.

We thought we could probably just go off grid and live in Wangi forever, as long as they never got internet coverage there. With zero internet we would have zero problems. We could sell the Outlander hire car, Cameron reasoned, and sell our phones, moving down to selling our tequila and half-finished rum. My god I must have been drunk last night, singing in the dark while Cameron went to get the rum, staring at the white frills of falls probably surrounded by crocodiles. Cameron is right, he is a rational man. We used 'boom' in a slightly unusual way, I think as an adjective, during our first night's night swim, which involved whiskey and nudity and the moon being too bright to see stars. 'That moon is boom,' I think it went. Near Litchfield Safari Camp on our second attempt to buy ice, I requested that the music be more boom and Cameron said, 'Lucy, do you really think I don't know what boom is?' I like that Cameron only told me as we were leaving that he was probably much more scared of swimming with crocs than I was; I hadn't noticed until that exact point. We talked about making decisions several times at the beginning of the road, and when Cameron invented a new type of breakfast toast involving cold pea and ham soup as a kind of smashed avocado replacement, he named it 'The Decision Maker'. We were never running late, we were never waiting. We both knew within 30 seconds that we should definitely leave Robin Falls and were back in the car in under five minutes. One day soon I should try to write down what the different days were. 'Blueys Blockhole' was what Buley Rockhole became. Our second time there we drank Dark and Stormy out of an old soda bottle (like a plastic Woolworths-brand bottle) – I drank most of it by accident – and watched a family of four kids dive into one of the top pools – one of the youngest boys never used his arms, which is to say he flung his little body out head first and it looked so great, and Cameron said he has developed a real knack for making the right cocktail for the right moment, and the sun was setting and I thought that was a nice thing to notice about himself and told him. Driving home the sun was still setting and it was so big and round and utterly crazy over the mountains of rocks and termite mounds and just as I tried to take its photo it was suddenly gone.

V

The errant, unaccountable notion I have about apocalypse is that it was the word that Ancient Greek sailors used to describe the exact moment in which they could no longer see land.

Sometimes I try to find out where I got it from.

It could have been Foucault, who is prone to exaggeration: 'Brothels, colonies are two extreme types of heterotopia, and if we think, after all, that the boat is a floating piece of space, a place without a place, that exists by itself and at the same time is given over to the infinity of the sea ...' ('Of Other Spaces: Utopias and Heterotopias').

I once heard someone say that this misunderstands the sea, exaggerates its expanse. At the time I thought, yes. Although the guy continued and said that this is what is imagined by those who stare at the water from the side. Those who stare at the water from the side see only the similarities of waves and sand. I realised I hated this little conversation we were having on the side. Seas are much like deserts, the guy said with conviction. They are not devoid of local character. We are not devoid of local character. How did we fare?

The term 'apocalypse' has its original meaning in the Greek *apo* (off, turn away from) + *calypso* (cover, or conceal): literally, the term means to uncover, or to unconceal, that is to say, to reveal – hence its biblical and Roman translation, 'revelation'.

As Kristeva observes, '*apocalypso* means dis-covering through sight, and contrasts with *alethia*, the philosophical disclosure of truth' (*Black Sun*).

In Homer's *Odyssey*, Calypso detained Odysseus on her island for seven years. Calypso's name derives from καλύπτω (*kalyptō*), meaning to cover, to conceal, to hide, or to deceive; καλύπτω is derived from the proto-Indo-European 'kel', making it cognate with the English 'hell'.

Calypso is a type of music originating in Trinidad and Tobago. According to scholars it does not share etymological roots with the mythical character Calypso; instead its roots are in the Efik *ka isu*, 'go on!' or in the corruption of the French *carrouseaux*. Yet the homonym, or pun, if it can be called that, is felicitous: it aptly describes the musical genre's political function in Afro-Caribbean society to disseminate masked meanings submerged in doublespeak: messages, news and plans between people who were slaves.

Anne Carson writes, 'A pun is a figure of language that depends on similarity of sound and disparity of meaning. It matches two sounds that fit perfectly together as aural shapes yet stand insistently, provocatively apart in sense. You perceive homophony and at the same time see the semantic space that separates the two words. Sameness is projected onto difference in a kind of stereoscopy. There is something irresistible in that' (*Eros the Bittersweet: An Essay*).

This is what George thinks: 'Etymologically speaking there is nothing in the word that refers to the sea, Luce.'

VI

How to begin a grammar lesson. 'Apostrophe' in Greek is *apo* (off, away from) + *strophe* (turn). An accent of elision in late Latin. Do you think one reason people confuse their apostrophes (fresh banana's, clean window's, you're problem) is that absence is very confusing? It's such a turn-off. I don't miss that. I immediately turn back to my business. Apostrophe expresses concern for the management of absence. Oh: I miss you. Do you have deep and mistaken feelings that belong to you?

Do you have the cleanest windows in the world? In the geography lesson's landscape, the images are real and still accessible. They come back clear.

Possession is a grammatical category. Contraction is a poetic category. Poetry is a possessive contraction.

The first year I lived here I would wait for Saturday to go and see you. I would drop my boyfriend off at his job, which was in a building behind Red Rooster in Richmond. His job was to organise old videotapes that the company had acquired from video stores that were going out of business. It seemed like this was the place where all these things could happen. The video-tapes were stored away for future use.

AUSTRALIAN
OPEN
I

I

I've never been happier than at the tennis today, my son and I sitting quietly, posed in our idea of gentlemen, applauding rallies and whispering 'out' or 'in' when Zhang challenged. Three hours and a ball, and the blue Plexicushion. And Show Court 3 in silence. My heart in the final game and I was as excited as the kids I joined at the boundary, holding my sharpie and autograph pad. Alison Riske came to me first. 'Thanks for coming to watch.' 'I love how you fight,' I answered.

Tennis has no time limit. The question, 'When does the match end?' makes no sense. Tennis just goes on. Like other things that are real, there is no limit. Except for the violations. If you have a problem with this, you don't like the good tennis. What is a better question? Why is it so hard to be at the right place at the right time?

The serve is the rhetorical question that I always answered.

To the birds who sing it, song is the aggressive claiming of territory. Australia is home to the world's loudest and most varied songbirds. It is believed that songbirds originated in Australia. It is believed that human song developed in mimicry of birds.

To watch this fight is to be immersed in the distraction. A bird slings by just before serve and is nearly hit by the receiver. My son pulls at his sock and then at his shoe. A ball kid scrapes behind a cricket.

The return is a consequence, it is not an answer. A return is a territorial swoop. There's more juice on the return.

I watched the neighbourhood wash by on the number 1 tram. I closed my eyes and saw Plexicushion blue. This racquet requires tension. More juice. More return.

II

The surface is the most important thing in tennis. The surface
determines the speed and bounce of the ball. The surface determines
the movement of the player coming to hit it.

We would like to show you the
specific steps to a court being
constructed. On site the work

begins. Frequently the
trees and foliage
have to be

removed from the
site. Due to
topography constraints,

excavation and suspension
are often necessary
to level the
playing area

To paint it all is a bit time-consuming. It's not automatic. Obviously.
You can see. It's not done by a machine. So. It's very hands-on. To
resurface the courts every year. To clean them with high pressure.

To then go through a process of three applications on every court.
Every court must be the same. It is all a bit labour-intensive. And
speed, speed is a critical part. Speed is the critical part. Labour is the
absolute. Speed is the absolute.

III

Or depict the Australian terrain. From a high angle, the camera records a scene into which a lone man enters. The commentary box: *déjà vu* all over again.

The man as *arriviste*. The man as case in point. An enigmatic figure that sometimes seems to be working. The man with the miles in his legs.

Flat through the court but a great redirector of the tennis ball, with 40 per cent of his wins against top tenners. He's playing about as well as he can without hitting a cold winner. The problem is, how long can he keep serving like that?

'Close the game! When it's 40–30!' At this moment, I write this sentence: Australians are more emotional now.

The court is a discursive space created by finding the first serve. The first game of the second set has taken on a huge significance. The fight is all-consuming. He introduces that drop shot. The errors are coming.

What does it all mean? A complex knowledge that turns on margins, constructed by planners and geographers. This image is structured around a vertical marker and a horizontal marker. Each centres the space. It is an unbelievable exchange. Gestures, numbers, averages, with the existence of general laws. Parity and unity. A taste of soil. A distant land.

I have an exemplary view. I am a cultivated observer.

He wanders onto the court. A topographical parenthesis, or rare, a charismatic Australian.

Describing a way of clairvoyance. The commentary box: I think it's a night we don't dwell on things: life moves on. I take small steps. Then I take a long stride with my foot on this idea.

IV

The Australian Open is on the left-hand television. On the middle
television is a three-minute loop that seems to feature a fitness app.
The right-hand television shows footage of a storm at sea. Then it
shows Manus Island detainees. The right-hand television seems to
feature more events than the television on the left and the television
in the middle. Why have a breakdown every summer? The left-hand
television shows highlights of Nadal's apology to a ball kid. Her face
caught a badly struck ball. I'm fine. I'm quite flushed. The girl is not
ready when Nadal apologises, strokes and kisses her face.

V

Even though it is the longest match he's ever played, we don't watch
Nick Kyrgios win his five-setter. We flick over to Medvedev and
Popyrin and contemplate skinny males instead. Medvedev plays the
ball flat when he wants to, and he knows how to run the back of the
court.

What makes this game appealing is that you can be way ahead for
a while. I am conscious of my house, of how it is tidy and quiet and
empty, and is my carpet acrylic? I move around its piles of books.
Fake underarm serve. Followed by the wrecking ball.

VI

I had not read *Letters Home* before. I had not had that kind of phase. My mum is downstairs with the tennis on the television. Or she is sitting somewhere else, waiting for me.

This is wrong of me, maybe. But I like Plath's escalating demands. Especially the way she escalates demands at the end of the book. Somewhere in her last letters she asks if her new sister-in-law, whom she'd never met, might come to England to help with the children. This is an example of how her major problem in life was access to affordable childcare.

In her letters Plath was upbeat until she died. So much of what she wrote was around this conditional: 'if I could only find a girl ...' and 'if I can just write uninterrupted for four hours a day'.

That time that family at the ice rink was next to me. The mother listening to her daughter's story, which was a complaint. There was some injustice about permission given or not given and a bathroom or a bathroom door. The mother listened and then discoursed to her daughter about the unhealthy nature of her relationship with her past. 'That's why we don't hold onto things from the past,' she closed.

VII

In the second men's semifinals, there are two beautiful males, *les beaux BOIS*, warming up the court.

After several minutes watching the player profiles, my mother says gravely, 'They're both very good looking.' We were determined to know these beings. This is a totally female principle of gratification, knowing beings. This was our daily work, this agricultural labour, curious all summer to make this surface produce this pulse.

Thoreau said he was determined to know beans – 'The Bean-Field' being a pun for 'the being field', this pun alluding to a relation to land set out by the georgic: being guaranteed by turning land to profit. Though he says, 'I was much slower and much more intimate with my beans than usual'. Here is the responsible non-dreamer working only for tropes and commentary in the only open and cultivated field. As I have little experience with this sort of work, there is not yet any commentary.

VIII

And then I say, 'Yeah, mum,' I say, 'I don't even know why I like this tennis.'

It must be mum. When we used to watch it, all those hours. Something to do with Perth summer, the necessary television.

Tennis. I explain how she said she hadn't been watching the Open when I asked her at the airport when I came to pick her up. I met her at the baggage carousel. I talk about how she doesn't remember some of the rules, how she doesn't recognise players, how she doesn't recognise the legends.

I explain that she was a club champion. Hold. I explain that she explained to me how her team just kept winning when they were all teens in the late 1970s. 'We just kept winning,' she said, as great a mystery to her as to anyone else. She couldn't say why they all decided to stop when they reached State. No one could say. One day she placed all her trophies outside.

I raise my left hand. I was born left-handed. I extend it as if to play a chord. Hold.

I can never raise it. No, you can never raise it, you can only be it.

AUSTRALIAN
OPEN
II

George's Door

For the cover of his debut collection of poetry, *Angel Frankenstein*, George Mouratidis selected a photograph of his parents' security screen door. In the photograph, a red flower (carnation or rose) is tucked into the aluminium frame, after a Greek custom of visiting that lives on in suburban Australia. The image speaks of an alien (to me) notion of visiting someone at home without calling ahead. For the idea is that the flower is left by the visitor on finding the people they intended to visit are not home.

I wonder why this is a difficult subject to write about, George's door, because I am close to George, or because George's dad died on Monday, or because I find nearly all subjects difficult to write about. I fight the urge, for instance, to include my observation that the visitor must travel with the pessimistic expectation they will find the house unattended – otherwise why would they have on hand the fresh flower? I silence speculation about whether the flower is fresh or fake, whether it is one of a bunch, and so on, because they seem off-topic. Because I know these speculations are somehow related to the unresolved status of my decision this week to send flowers to George's house, or something else, or nothing.

Really, I'm interested in the door. This type of security door lets the light in, but shields the people indoors from the view of those outdoors. Standing outside this screen door a visitor would not be able to tell whether the other door (usually made of wood or other solid stuff) was open or closed without pressing their face against the metallic mesh, which from memory smells of dust and rain. Solid door open, face pressed against the mesh of the closed security door, the visitor might catch an outline or shadow of someone inside.

It is a deformed introductory gesture, this door of George's (or is it this door of mine?). I know I am using this door for another purpose, which is to talk about desire. I want to say this is an Ovidian image.

The rose or carnation tucked into the aluminium, or the visitor – pressing their face against the screen, blinking to see shadow fall within?

At the funeral, George reads some poetry by Yannis Ritsos, his father's favourite poet. Maybe George's favourite poet. An enlightening moment is when one of George's Thomastown friends, Costas, says to me in passing, 'If you don't know George's dad, you can't understand George.' The mourners place a red carnation in the coffin. I take a red carnation with me from the chapel. I realise with surprise that I already have a vase full of red carnations at home, which have been opening over three weeks. One of the poems, in English translation, has a line about where a shadow will always fall. How hard the hard work of our fathers presses.

I didn't go back to the house (I don't know why). I came here to write this instead. It only occurs to me now that if I had gone, I would have had a good look at that door. My fascination with this door is irrational, because there is nothing exceptional about a door like this. Many suburban houses built in Australia have this door. The house I grew up in, for instance. Strangely, I realise much later, so does the house I live in now. There is nothing strange about this. This is a standard Australian door.

Bush Poem

Every land is a way of speaking
every way of speaking is a land
even in this oppression
I a stake in some mad fence
impound this land: no

I thought create nothing, defeat the purpose
leave the trees there
leave the leaves there
leave
don't recall any names

Turn around or turn loose
where I or you or some third person
some terrible smart cunt
go into the countryside
even though walking is clearing

I a mast stupidly seafaring
all I in the mountain's oceans
all door in the commons
open doors are commas
slammed doors are exclamation marks
broken off the frame a slash
a sliding door one kind of dash

Asterisk a little chip on my shoulder

Footnotes the witty shoes
I tripped in all the way to meet you

I thought I could be a house
that I never fix or leave
that I could annexe

I am very much over-introducing things
and, of course, very pleased to meet you
in this extended preface
you have a beautiful face
especially behind this door, where I stand
In infinite regress with the doorkeeper
I bloody love a good door
where did you get it?
how does it sound when it opens and shuts?

Left open
I thought like a tree
like a nation of trees
I don't know its name
I come here again
before I leave you my address
in water and dissolution
in the shadow of a bulldozer or man from the country
in his property by logical procedure

Leaves

It is time for brunch. I find myself in the landscape of a devouring multitude. What is brunch? 'No!' she said. 'There was no such thing!' Couples wonder in never-ending phones. Workers count in side businesses. Vegetables colour. Maybe I can live on carrots. I can count on carrots as my side business. Lucy Van. Lucy Of. A very silly little name. If you look at only one side of it. There is the other side. A Little Cloud. I am using the word 'sanctimonious' on a nearly daily basis. My son noticing my mother's schizophrenia, well, my alarm incalculable. How sanity comes and goes. Treats a person like a hotel. Hotels are not romantic or artistic but I think maybe they are transcendent. The corruption of one thing is the creation of another. I think; it is said. My simple dream to write one decent thing about one decent person. I.e. I want to be good. DASHED. Now I dash into kitsch. Or is it the kitchen, is this more kitsch? I think of my mother every day. Mum, I think of you every day. My thoughts are containers. I leave half-eaten fruit in rooms. My child is the boss and the fault of mine. I revive my Italian. I am essentially a shithead; my favourite part of the day was deciding that potatoes are not really vegetables. This is what we are like, what we like, we like being shitheads. Digestive tract möbius stripping. Shitheads: well, are we doing this? I hate the word 'veggies' but I don't mind the word 'veg'. But I definitely hate the word 'space', maybe even more than I hate the word 'veggies'. I love the word 'containers' and I love the word 'attack' and I love the word 'smoko'.

Somewhere scales are practised by husband and wife harpists. Emotions are guided reactions, she is told by him. All forms of authority are rejected by her. To embody or project it is refused by her. The passive voice is loved by them. Something sexy in their cat killing birds. They're only Indian myna birds, they're not natives. That's what the harpists say. The harpists find the soft bird bodies half-eaten in different parts of the courtyard, near the potato plant, near the hose. Preludes to throat clearing. She thinks: incipit: always be opening. The concept of a dead language. She is an old woman and he is a lover of old women.

Such a woman's drawer, crusted pyjamas and pregnancy tests and empty boxes of valium. For me you'll go, for I am Beatrice. Recondite working-class shithead, here I go, or come: but if you think I slept my way here you don't even know that I'm not even good in bed (this is a lie). I won't tell you about the literary mole that interviewed me, a classically trained harpist: 'And you just used the word trope. And what is a trope?' I meant to say 'pianist' but I changed it you see. Oh I am a bitter veg a little working-class girl slipping on that crossing ferry. I must tell someone I ate a whole loaf of garlic bread for breakfast. Cameron, my Cameron, I ate a whole loaf of garlic bread for breakfast. Oh it was great. I never think of Walt Whitman (this is a lie) but I wonder what Whitman would have said about brunch? And I wonder, is it worth wondering this? Say what you want about Whitman, but he had those leadership skills and appetites and liked people and liked what they liked, or maybe he knew how to talk to them or maybe he knew what they wanted to hear and maybe it's all that it takes, that profane communication biblical never-ending.

Let him lead where? Out of position the harpists drive to arcadia. They stand in a field. The wife returns to the car to look for cut flowers she knows aren't there. Improbably there is a plastic blue rosary that she takes and leaves on the stone in the shape of a refined tree. A couple of centuries ago someone came and cut down the trees and planted grass. If you were wondering, grass is powerful social control. A child said, what is grass? Fetching it to me with full hands. And now it seems to me the uncut hair of graves. The harpists read, 'What is grass' on a poetry website. They scroll through the user comments. 'I love it! You should keep writing!' someone encourages

Walt. And the harpists wonder, what is apostrophe? I think of Marianne Moore all the time. When Elizabeth Bishop took her walking through Brooklyn, Bishop said, 'Marianne, we are standing on the corner where Walt Whitman lived,' and Moore said, 'Elizabeth! *Never* speak to me of that man!' *Never speak to me of that man.* But that wording might be wrong, because I am always losing my Bishop. That is not a chess reference. None of this has anything to do with chess. That is a reference to inaccurate Bishop referencing. All of this has a lot to do with inaccurately and constantly losing my Bishop.

The Malouf

One time I even thought I would respond to David Malouf. For a couple of years, I wandered around different places in Melbourne and sometimes even other places with a copy of that *Quarterly Essay* piece, 'Made in England'. It was a photocopy; I couldn't find the original. It was held together with a bulldog clip; I couldn't find a stapler.

Because the copy was like this, and not in a book, or in a folder, or in a computer, it was easy to carry around with me. I kept it. It's soft with dust. It's still with me. It is here.

I had an issue with his handling of documents. Which isn't to say that he wasn't careful. Actually, I am saying that it bothers me that he handles documents with great delicacy. He carefully describes how the librarian at the Folger Library, 'in those humming vaults', shows him and two other (Malouf uses the word 'fellow', which makes me think he really meant 'fallow') Australian writers the world's most complete collection of Shakespeariana.

The idea of the sacred text fills the writer with that Maloufian glee:

> For her this is the real centre of the city and what it stands for: the power of what is memorialised but also embodied here, the spirit of the language we share: all that is contained in these sacred texts and in what, over the past three centuries, they have gathered about them … their extraordinary hold on the mind and the magnetic force of their influence. This is what will survive down here should the surrounding empire, like so many before it, crumble and blow away

These sacred texts.

Folio, whereart thou? I am in the Folger Library. I am always taken through special collections. Humming, I perform the proper responses when I'm shown this rare document or that special document. I improvise opinions and awe. Though I want to go outside. I want to go back to my Washington hotel, to be very bored in a different way.

The idea that there are sacred texts makes me think of all the poetry books I bought for a dollar or found on a 'for free' shelf or had thrust onto me by their authors to save them from pulping. These are the books I have found myself writing about.

These are also sacred texts. Not because they are 'just as important' or their voices 'as valid' or 'needing to be heard' as Shakespeare's works. They are sacred books in the same way the Folger's Shakespeariana is sacred. They share a certain way of being outside literature. These are the texts that nobody touches. They cannot be exchanged in the normal commercial ways. They are never in the normal part of the library. They have something to do with being contaminated. They are outside.

I wrote somewhere: 'poetry is the negation of emplotment'. But I think I meant to say: poetry is the negation of employment. Which is to say that what people make from the sales of their poetry books is an oddly kept secret.

It's difficult to see the connection between the sacred text and the brutal act. When it comes to origins this is unrecounted. What I mean is that when it comes to origins, this connection is barred from view. It is outside. This remains barred in perfect form in Malouf's essay 'Made in England'.

Oh, I had a good laugh when I read it.

~

The place where Malouf's narratorial discretion gives way is the library. The most vivid memory I have of *Johnno* is of his description of all the men using the State Library of Queensland.

I went to the local library in Box Hill on a whim. I had met Laila near Box Hill station. She smoked a cigarette while I bought a takeaway coffee. We walked and coming out of lockdown we were touched by what she later described as relics of the human interaction we took for granted. 'Wow, a park bench!' 'A half-functioning library!' 'A dance school on the median strip!'

The park bench had armrests that were made into a pair of sphinxes carved in white stone.

When we arrived the security guard took our temperatures and our names and numbers. We were brought inside, where a librarian explained that we were not to sit down or browse. We could stay no longer than 30 minutes. We briefly admired the spines of their philosophy collection; their collection on Chinese history. We moved on to the exit, where the Box Hill Historical Society keeps their glass cabinet. For a moment we both mistook a black-and-white photograph of a group of women, wearing uniform suits and berets, for the historical society itself.

Because It's Slower It Races Away

Someone at the place that used to be Michel's Patisserie but is now called something else and is in fact something entirely else but despite efforts seems more generic than Michel's Patisserie with its new mint-green and blond wood is wearing a red 'Free Julian Assange' shirt. Maybe 12 years ago I saw Julian Assange walk right from where I'm standing to the counter of Woolworths, which might have been called Safeway back then but was essentially the same place as it is now even down to the lighting system buy or request to buy a SIM card for a prepaid mobile phone. That's Julian Assange, I thought. He is buying a SIM card for a prepaid mobile phone. I knew as much about him then as today, which aside from the words 'Internet' and 'Freedom' is zero despite or perhaps because of the fact I once watched a poorly made biopic about his early life in Melbourne. Something about Dandenong, or is it the Dandenongs. Good at the Internet. Something to do with war and America. Or is it sex and Sweden. The Internet, which I can't explain but am always on or is it always in except for when I sleep and being in the Internet is so like being asleep or is it a dream. I'm here because I've been working my way up to this moment. Not that there's anything wrong with me, or wrong with this Shopping Centre. There is, but that isn't the point. The point is I need to buy thrush medication to treat the UTI medication to treat the unprotected sex, which I suppose I had as a treat. Chemist Warehouse of course is a dream and a curse to the germaphobes and to the racists and the way I live in the Internet is like the way I live in the coronavirus, perfectly well in those correlative ways without understanding anything at all about it but receiving this information or is it this dream. Life ebbing or is it flaring in Chemist Warehouse, a fact of life I ascribe to the general paranoia between the different customers and between the customers and the staff though I don't feel paranoia between the staff themselves. Weeks later I'll see the security guard remember and describe what will seem like one of his big nights to the young woman behind the checkout counter. I'm not surprised there's some aggression between an old man on his bicycle and an unseeable driver in a grey vehicle and I take the aggression on board because it feels like mine to take. Even though I only came for the thrush medication my backpack has other items I purchased and took from Chemist Warehouse and also Woolworths including: a Twix, a surprisingly square carrot, an expensive coconut water I didn't want. I have been working up to this moment or is it that this moment has taken a lot of effort. I didn't want this moment or is it that I don't understand this moment. It is aggressive, expensive, sick with this moment, this moment, or is it that I'm here.

ACKNOWLEDGEMENTS

An early version of 'Leaves' appeared in *Australian Poetry Anthology* (2018).

I want to thank my extended and immediate family – most especially my mother, my father, my sister – for everything.

I want to thank Bella Li for her editorial work. You are simply astounding, and I am simply so grateful. I also thank Anne Maxwell: this book redirects years of research in anti-colonialism, postcolonialism and the history of photography, which you have supported in many ways. I also thank Noel King for the vitally important books he sends.

For their encouragement to contribute to Australian writing I really want to thank Justin Clemens, Kent MacCarter (a thousand times), Michelle Cahill and, right at the beginning, Hoa Pham. And I have special thanks for Evelyn Araluen: thank you for making that important phone call at the beginning of 2020.

I also thank organisations including Sick Leave, Sporting Poets, *Overland*, the Wheeler Centre and the NGV, for providing space for me to conceive and share this work in its early phases. And I thank the City of Melbourne for supporting the realisation of this work with its 2020 Quick Response Arts Grant.

I thank those I have collaborated with on intense, special projects in the past: Laila Sakini, Autumn Royal and Dallas Phillips. I have learnt a lot by listening and feeling with you. For all their special ways, I thank Ruth McIver, Melanie Thomson, George Mouratidis, Cameron Hill, Tina LaRocca, Gemma Blackwood, Melissa Newby, Ling Toong and Angela Hesson.

A special thank you to Leo Thomson for the wild, gimmick-free thoughts I often steal. And, most of all, I thank Freddy, who is endless.

Lucy Van writes poetry and criticism. She teaches literary studies at the University of Melbourne, where she has also been a Melbourne Research Fellow. In 2019 and 2020, she was a writer in residence at *Overland Literary Journal*. *Figures*, her spoken poetry EP, was produced in collaboration with musician Laila Sakini and released by Purely Physical (UK) in 2017. Her work has appeared in publications including *History of Photography*, *Journal of Australian Studies*, *Southerly*, *Axon: Creative Explorations*, *Cordite Poetry Review*, *Australian Poetry Journal*, *The Suburban Review*, *Mascara Literary Review*, *Peril Magazine* and *Arc Poetry Magazine*.